DOVER ☆ CHILDREN'S THRIFT CLASSICS

The Adventures of Sammy Jay

THORNTON W. BURGESS

Original Illustrations by Harrison Cady

PUBLISHED IN ASSOCIATION WITH THE
THORNTON W. BURGESS MUSEUM AND THE
GREEN BRIAR NATURE CENTER, SANDWICH, MASSACHUSETTS,
BY
DOVER PUBLICATIONS, INC., MINEOLA, NEW YORK

DOVER CHILDREN'S THRIFT CLASSICS

EDITOR OF THIS VOLUME: JANET BAINE KOPITO

Copyright

Bibliographical Note

This Dover edition, first published in 2006 in association with the Thornton W. Burgess Museum and the Green Briar Nature Center, Sandwich, Massachusetts, who have provided a new introduction, is an unabridged republication of the work first published by Little, Brown, and Company, Boston, in 1915. It contains the original Harrison Cady illustrations.

Library of Congress Cataloging-in-Publication Data

Burgess, Thornton W. (Thornton Waldo), 1874–1965.
  The adventures of Sammy Jay / Thornton W. Burgess ; original illustrations by Harrison Cady.
    p. cm.—(Dover children's thrift classics)
  "Published in association with the Thornton W. Burgess Museum and the Green Briar Nature Center, Sandwich, Massachusetts."
  Summary: Relates the adventures of Sammy Jay, a lazy bird who would rather steal from his neighbors than find his own food.
  ISBN-13: 978-0-486-44946-3 (pbk.)
  ISBN-10: 0-486-44946-7 (pbk.)
  [1. Blue jay—Fiction. 2. Birds—Fiction. 3. Forest animals—Fiction. 4. Forests and forestry—Fiction.] I. Cady, Harrison, 1877– ill. II. Title. III. Series.

PZ7.B917Ah 2006
[Fic]—dc22
                                                              2005056931

Manufactured in the United States by Courier Corporation
44946704   2013
www.doverpublications.com

Introduction to the Dover Edition

Winter is approaching, and although Sammy Jay does not mind the cold, he does not like the fact that he has to work hard to find food. You see, Sammy Jay is quite a lazy fellow, and he hardly likes to work at all—in fact, instead of working, he watches his neighbors in order to find where they store their food, and he steals it! Not only is Sammy Jay lazy, but he also is very sly, and is a troublemaker. He takes great pleasure in making trouble in the Briar Patch and Green Forest. Chatterer the Squirrel is quite clever himself, and he does not like to be outwitted. Chatterer is storing his sweet acorns for the winter, and who do you think is watching, or should we say, spying? Sammy Jay, of course! As you read this delightful book you will find out how Chatterer and Sammy play tricks on and outwit each other. Can you guess who gets the last laugh?

The Adventures of Sammy Jay was first published back in 1915. Sammy Jay appears in many of the stories written by Thornton W. Burgess. Mr. Burgess wrote over 170 books for children, about all different kinds of animals. Thornton W. Burgess grew up in Sandwich, Massachusetts, a small town on Cape Cod. He started out by writing stories for his own young son, and he became a famous author. He also wrote a newspaper column and published over 15,000 newspaper stories, called "The Bedtime Stories." This column ran for more than 50 years.

Mr. Burgess was also the host of a radio program called "The Radio Nature League." Through his books, newspaper columns, and radio programs, Mr. Burgess taught millions of children to love and respect nature. Today, the Thornton W. Burgess Society carries on this tradition. The Society is a nonprofit environmental-education organization located in Sandwich. The Society operates the Thornton W. Burgess Museum and the Green Briar Nature Center, and it manages the East Sandwich Game Farm. You can learn more about the Thornton W. Burgess Society and its facilities by visiting our web site: www.thorntonburgess.org.

Contents

List of Illustrations

vii

I
Sammy Jay Makes a Fuss

SAMMY JAY doesn't mind the cold of winter. Indeed, he rather likes it. Under his handsome coat of blue, trimmed with white, he wears a warm, silky suit of underwear, and he laughs at rough Brother North Wind and his cousin, Jack Frost. But still he doesn't like the winter as well as he does the warmer seasons because—well, because he is a lazy fellow and doesn't like to work for a living any harder than he has to, and in the winter it isn't so easy to get something to eat.

And there is another reason why Sammy Jay doesn't like the winter as well as the other seasons. What do you think it is? It isn't a nice reason at all. No, Sir, it isn't a nice reason at all. It is because it isn't so easy to stir up trouble. Somehow, Sammy Jay never seems really happy unless he is stirring up trouble for someone else. He just delights in tormenting other little people of the Green Meadows and the Green Forest.

Dear, dear, it is a dreadful thing to say, but Sammy Jay is bold and bad. He steals! Yes, Sir, Sammy Jay steals whenever he gets a chance. He would rather steal a breakfast anytime than get it honestly. Now people who steal usually are very

1

sly. Sammy Jay is sly. Indeed, he is one of the slyest of all the little people who live in the Green Forest. Instead of spending his time honestly hunting for his meals, he spends most of it watching his neighbors to find out where they have their storehouses, so that he can help himself when their backs are turned. He slips through the Green Forest as still as still can be, hiding in the thick treetops and behind the trunks of big trees, and peering out with those sharp eyes of his at his neighbors. Whenever he is discovered, he always pretends to be very busy about his own business, and very much surprised to find anyone is near.

It was in this way that he had discovered one of the storehouses of Chatterer the Red Squirrel. He didn't let Chatterer know that he had discovered it. Oh, my, no! He didn't even go near it again for a long time. But he didn't forget it. Sammy Jay never forgets things of that kind, never! He thought of it often and often. When he did, he would say to himself:

> "Sometime when the snow is deep
>   And Chatterer is fast asleep,
>   When Mother Nature is unkind
>   And things to eat are hard to find,
>   I'll help myself and fly away
>   To steal again some other day."

The snow was deep now, and things to eat were hard to find, but Chatterer the Red Squirrel wasn't asleep. No, indeed! Chatterer seemed to like the cold weather and was as frisky and spry as ever he is. And he never went very far away from that storehouse. Sammy Jay watched and watched, but never once did he get a chance to steal the sweet acorns that he had seen Chatterer store away in the fall.

"H-m-m!" said Sammy Jay to himself, "I must do something to get Chatterer away from his store-house."

For a long time Sammy Jay sat in the top of a tall, dark pine tree, thinking and thinking. Then his sharp eyes twinkled with a look of great cunning, and he chuckled. It was a naughty chuckle. Away he flew to a very thick spruce tree some distance away in the Green Forest, but where Chatterer the Red Squirrel could hear him. There Sammy Jay began to make a great fuss. He screamed and screeched as only he can. Pretty soon, just as he expected, he saw Chatterer the Red Squirrel hurrying over to see what the fuss was all about. Sammy Jay slipped out of the other side of the spruce tree and without a sound hurried over to Chatterer's storehouse.

As he flew through the Green Forest, Sammy Jay
chuckled and chuckled to himself. *See page 5.*

II
A Bitter Disappointment

AS he flew through the Green Forest, Sammy Jay chuckled and chuckled to himself. It wasn't a good chuckle to hear. It was the kind of chuckle that only folks who are doing wrong, and think they are smart because they are doing wrong, use. Sammy Jay thought that he was smart, very smart indeed. He had screamed and shrieked and made a great fuss over nothing at all until Chatterer the Red Squirrel had come hurrying over to find out what it all meant. Then Sammy Jay had slipped away unseen and come straight to the storehouse of Chatterer the Red Squirrel.

This particular storehouse had once been the home of Blacky the Crow. When Blacky deserted it for a new home, Chatterer had taken it for a storehouse. He had roofed it over, and all through the pleasant fall he had stored away nuts and acorns in it. Sammy Jay had watched him. He had seen those sweet acorns and nuts put there, and he had never forgotten them. Now, with the snow deep on the ground, the easiest way to get a good meal that he knew of was to steal some of those very acorns. So he chuckled as he pulled apart the roof of Chatterer's storehouse in search of those acorns.

Now Chatterer the Red Squirrel is quite as smart as Sammy Jay. Indeed, he is very much like Sammy Jay, for he is a mischief-maker and a thief himself. So, because people who do wrong always are on the watch for others to do wrong, Chatterer the Red Squirrel had kept his sharp eyes wide open all the time he had been filling his storehouse in the fall, and he had spied Sammy Jay's smart blue coat when Sammy had thought himself nicely hidden. Chatterer had known what Sammy Jay was hiding there for. His sharp eyes snapped, but he went right on filling his storehouse just the same. Then, just as soon as he was sure that Sammy Jay had gone away, Chatterer had taken out every one of the sweet acorns and put them in another storehouse inside a hollow tree. He had left nothing but hickory nuts, for he knew that these are too hard for Sammy Jay to crack.

But Sammy Jay didn't know anything about this, and so now, as he broke his way into the storehouse, he chuckled greedily. Pretty soon he had a hole big enough to stick his head in, and his mouth watered as he reached in for a sweet acorn. All he could find were hard hickory nuts. What did it mean? In a great rage, Sammy Jay began to tear the storehouse to pieces. There must be some sweet acorns there somewhere! Hadn't he seen Chatterer put them there? He forgot that he was stealing. He forgot everything except his disappointment, and the more he thought of this, the angrier he grew.

He would have pulled the storehouse all to pieces, if Chatterer himself hadn't come home.

Sammy Jay had just stopped for breath when he heard the rattle of claws on the bark of the tree. He knew what that meant, and he didn't wait to look down. He just spread his blue wings and with a scream of rage flew over to the next tree. Then such a dreadful noise as there was in the Green Forest!

"Robber!" screamed Chatterer the Red Squirrel, dancing up and down with anger.

"Thief yourself!" screamed Sammy Jay.

It was a dreadful quarrel, and all the little forest people who were within hearing stopped their ears.

HARRISON CADY

"Thief yourself!" screamed Sammy Jay. *See page 7.*

III
The Vanity of Sammy Jay

WHEN Sammy Jay isn't planning mischief, or sticking his bill into the affairs of other folks with which he has no concern, or trying to frighten someone bigger than himself or scare someone smaller than himself, he spends a great deal of his time admiring his fine clothes and thinking what a handsome fellow he is. And he is a handsome fellow. Even Chatterer the Red Squirrel, who is always quarreling with him, admits that Sammy Jay is a handsome fellow. He carries himself proudly when he thinks anyone is looking. His shape is very trim and neat, and he is a very smart-looking fellow indeed. And his coat! Was there ever such a coat before? It seems as if Old Mother Nature must have cut off a little piece of the sky when it was bluest on a summer day to make Sammy Jay's coat, and that she must have taken a tiny strip from the whitest cloud to trim it with. And then she gave him a smart cap and a black collar and a waistcoat of just the softest grayish white, that shows off his blue coat best. Old Mother Nature certainly was feeling very good indeed when she planned Sammy Jay's clothes.

Now Sammy Jay knows just how handsome he

9

is. If you should ask him, and he would condescend to talk to you at all, which he probably wouldn't do, he would tell you that he is the handsomest fellow in the world. Of course, this isn't true, but Sammy Jay thinks it is. And so Sammy Jay is very fond of showing off his fine clothes and making fun of other people who are not so finely dressed. He spends a great deal of time in caring for his beautiful coat and in admiring himself whenever he can see his reflection in a little pool of water.

Now Peter Rabbit isn't the least bit like Sammy Jay. He doesn't think about his clothes at all. Indeed, Peter thinks so little about his clothes that it doesn't trouble him a bit to wear a white patch on the seat of his trousers. And Peter dearly loves to make fun of Sammy Jay.

So it tickled Peter immensely one day to find Sammy Jay admiring himself. Peter had come up through the Green Forest without making a sound, for with the snow covering the ground, there were no dead leaves to rustle. As usual, his long ears were cocked up to catch every sound. Suddenly Peter stopped. He had heard Sammy Jay's voice, and by the sound, Peter knew that Sammy was talking to himself. Very, very softly Peter stole forward and hid where he could see Sammy Jay in a big pine tree.

"I've got the handsomest coat in all the Green Forest!" said Sammy Jay, stretching one of his wings out and cocking his head on one side to admire it. "And where else is such a beautiful tail to be found?" He spread his tail so that a ray of sunshine would fall on it. It certainly was very beautiful, as blue as the sky, with a little band of white across the tip and little bars of black across the outer sides. Even Peter Rabbit, with his nose turned up in scorn, had to admit to himself that it certainly was a handsome tail.

"I'm so glad it's mine!" sighed Sammy Jay. "It must be dreadful not to be handsome."

Peter Rabbit could keep still no longer. "It's a good thing you admire yourself, Sammy Jay, because no one else does!" he shouted.

> "Handsome is as it may do!
> Don't forget that, Sammy Jay.
> Underneath that coat of blue
> Is a black heart, Sammy Jay.
> Everybody near and far
> Knows you for just what you are—
> Of all mischief-makers chief.
> Handsome clothes won't hide a thief."

Sammy Jay flew into a rage, but when he opened his mouth to call Peter names, all he could say was "Thief! thief! thief!"

"What did I tell you?" said Peter Rabbit, grinning.

IV
Sammy Jay Gets Even with Peter Rabbit

"I'LL get even with you, Peter Rabbit! I'll get even with you!" Sammy Jay fairly hopped up and down on the branch of the big pine, he was so angry. Peter just thrust his tongue into one cheek in the sauciest way and then laughed at Sammy Jay. Of course, it is true, as everyone in the Green Forest and on the Green Meadows knows, that Sammy Jay is a thief. But no one likes to be told that he is a thief, even if he is, Sammy Jay least of all. Like a great many other people who do wrong, Sammy Jay likes to pretend that he is a very fine gentleman, and he wants other people to think so too. So he takes care of his handsome blue coat and struts around a great deal when he thinks other folks are looking at him.

So Sammy Jay studied and studied how he could get even with Peter Rabbit. He called Peter names whenever he saw him, but Peter didn't mind that in the least, for he could call names back again. Besides, names never hurt, and it is very foolish to call them. So Sammy Jay studied and studied and studied how he could get even with Peter Rabbit in some other way. Then one day, as he sat in the big pine tree studying, Sammy heard a voice that gave

12

HARRISON CADY

"I'll get even with you, Peter Rabbit!" *See page 12.*

him an idea. It was the voice of Redtail the Hawk, who, you know, is own cousin to old Whitetail and to Roughleg. Now Sammy Jay can scream so exactly like Redtail the Hawk that you cannot tell their voices apart. When he heard that scream, Sammy Jay chuckled out loud. He had thought of a plan to get even with Peter Rabbit.

Every day after that, Sammy Jay went peeking and prying through the Green Forest and around the edge of the Green Meadows without making a sound, just watching for Peter Rabbit. The snow was almost all gone, and that is how it happened that Redtail had come back from the South where he had spent the winter. Sammy Jay felt quite sure that Peter didn't know that Redtail was back yet. He hoped he didn't, anyway.

Early one morning, Sammy Jay sat hidden on the edge of the Green Forest, watching the Old Briar-patch where Peter Rabbit lives. He saw Peter come out of one of his private little paths and sit up very straight. For a long time Peter sat looking this way and looking that way over the Green Meadows. When he was sure that Reddy and Granny Fox were nowhere about, and that Roughleg was nowhere in sight, Peter kicked up his heels and scampered out on to the Green Meadows away from the dear Old Briar-patch to see if there were any signs of spring.

Sammy waited until Peter had reached the big hickory tree over by the Smiling Pool, then very silently he flew over to the big hickory tree. Peter was so busy looking for Jerry Muskrat that he didn't see Sammy Jay at all. Suddenly, right over Peter's head, sounded a fierce, shrill scream. Peter knew that voice. At least, he thought he did. He didn't stop to look. He had learned long ago that it is best to run first and look afterward. So now he started for the dear Old Briar-patch as fast as his long legs would take him, his heart in his mouth.

Again that fierce scream sounded right over him. Peter ran faster than ever, and as he ran, he dodged this way and dodged that way. Every second he expected to feel the sharp claws of Redtail the Hawk. My, such jumps as Peter did take! It seemed to him that he never would reach the dear Old Briar-patch. But he did, and just as soon as he was safely inside, he turned around to see what had become of Redtail. And what do you think he saw? Why, only Sammy Jay laughing fit to kill himself.

"Fraidcat! Fraidcat!" shouted Sammy Jay.

Peter shook his fist. Then he grinned foolishly. "I guess you are even, Sammy Jay!" he said.

V
Sammy Jay Brings News

PETER RABBIT had a very funny feeling. He had started out that morning with the best intentions in the world. He had meant to go straight to Chatterer the Red Squirrel and tell him how mean he had been to spy and so find the new house that Chatterer was trying to keep a secret, and then he had overheard Chatterer telling Tommy Tit the Chickadee how he had fooled Peter, and that Peter didn't know where the new house was, at all. Peter had never felt more foolish in his life. No, Sir, he never had felt more foolish in his life. Of course, if it were true that he had been fooled and really didn't know where Chatterer's new house was, there was no use in begging Chatterer's pardon, for he would only make himself still more of a laughing stock than he was already. And yet the thing he had done was just as mean as if he had found out Chatterer's secret, and he knew that he would feel better if he owned up. He scratched his left ear with his right hind foot and then scratched his right ear with his left hind foot. He pulled his whiskers, and still he didn't know what to do.

He was still trying to decide, when he heard a great racket in the direction of the Green Forest. It was Sammy Jay, screaming noisily as usual, and he was hurrying straight up to the Old Orchard. Of course, Chatterer heard him, and as soon as Sammy was within hearing, he called to him. Sammy hurried over at once.

"So here you are!" he exclaimed. "I've hunted all through the Green Forest for you until I'm quite tuckered out. I've got news for you."

"What is it?" begged Chatterer, dancing about with impatience.

"I've seen Shadow the Weasel," replied Sammy.

"Where is he?" asked Chatterer, and his voice sounded very anxious.

"He's over in the Green Forest, and he says he is going to stay there until he catches you, if he has to stay all winter," replied Sammy. "He says he is going to find you if he has to hunt through every tree in the Green Forest."

Chatterer actually turned pale for a minute. "You—you didn't tell him that I wasn't in the Green Forest, did you?" he asked.

"Of course I didn't! How could I when I didn't know it myself?" retorted Sammy scornfully.

"And—and you won't tell him when you see him again, will you, Sammy?" begged Chatterer.

"What do you take me for?" demanded Sammy angrily. "I haven't got any love for you, Chatterer, and you know it. You're a redheaded, red-coated nuisance, and I'm not a bit sorry to see you in trouble, but I wouldn't turn my worst enemy over to

"He's over in the Green Forest," replied Sammy.
See page 17.

such a cruel, cold-blooded robber as Shadow the
Weasel. He would kill me just as quickly as he
would you, if he could catch me, which he can't,
and I am going to make it my business to see to it
that all the little people who are afraid of him know
that he is about. I am going over to the Old Briar-
patch right away to warn Peter Rabbit."

"You don't need to, because I am right here,"
spoke up Peter from his hiding place. "I am ever so
much obliged to you for planning to warn me, and
I'm sorry I've ever said mean things about you,
Sammy Jay."

"Pooh!" replied Sammy. "You needn't be. I guess
I've deserved them."

Then Sammy and Peter and Chatterer began to
talk over the news about Shadow the Weasel so
eagerly that not one of them saw Black Pussy stealing along the old stone wall.

VI
Black Pussy Almost Catches a Good Breakfast

BLACK PUSSY was out very early, hunting for her breakfast. Not that she needed to hunt for her breakfast; oh, my, no! Black Pussy didn't need a single thing. Every morning Farmer Brown's boy filled a saucer with warm fresh milk for her, and every day she had all the meat that was good for her, so there wasn't the least need in the world for her to go hunting. Black Pussy was just like all cats. Lying before the fire in Farmer Brown's house, blinking and purring contentedly, she seemed too good-natured and gentle to hurt anyone, and all Farmer Brown's family said that she was and believed it. They knew nothing about the empty little nests in the joyful springtime—empty because Black Pussy had found them and emptied them and broken the hearts of little father and mother birds.

You see, Farmer Brown's folks really didn't know Black Pussy. But the little forest and meadow people did. They knew that Black Pussy was just like all cats—fierce and cruel down inside—and they hated Black Pussy, every one of them. They knew that down in her heart was the love of killing, just that same love of killing that is in the heart of Shad-

20

ow the Weasel, and so they hated Black Pussy. If she had had to hunt for a living, they wouldn't have minded so much, but she didn't have to hunt for a living, and so they hated her.

This particular morning Black Pussy had chosen to have a look along the old stone wall at the edge of the Old Orchard. Many times she had hunted Striped Chipmunk there. She didn't know enough about the ways of the little people of the Green Forest and the Green Meadows to know that this cold weather had sent Striped Chipmunk down into his snug bedroom underground for a long sleep, so she sneaked along from stone to stone, hoping that she would surprise him. She had gone half the length of the old wall without a sign of anything to catch when she heard voices that put all thought of Striped Chipmunk out of her head. Crawling flat on her stomach to keep out of sight, she softly worked nearer and nearer until, peeping from behind a big stone in the old wall, she could see Chatterer the Red Squirrel, Peter Rabbit, and Sammy Jay talking so busily and so excited that they didn't seem to be paying attention to anything else.

Sammy Jay was safe, because he was sitting in an old apple tree, but Chatterer was on the old wall, and Peter was on the ground. Which should she catch? Peter would make the biggest and best breakfast, but Black Pussy hadn't forgotten the terrible kick he had once given her when she had

Harrison Cady

This cold weather had sent Striped Chipmunk
underground for a long sleep. *See page 21.*

caught little Miss Fuzzytail up in the Old Pasture, and she had great respect for Peter's stout hind legs. She would be content to catch Chatterer this morning. She hated him, anyway, for he had been very saucy to her many times. He would never make fun of her or call her names again.

More slowly and carefully than ever, Black Pussy stole forward. Her eyes grew yellow with excitement, and fierce and cruel. At last she reached a place where one good jump would land her on Chatterer. Carefully she drew her feet under her to make the jump. The end of her black tail twitched with eagerness. Just as she got ready to spring, there was a shrill scream from Sammy Jay. He caught sight of the moving tip of that tail, and he knew what it meant. Black Pussy sprang, but she was just too late. Chatterer had dived headfirst down between the stones of the old wall at the sound of Sammy's scream, and Peter had dived headfirst into Johnny Chuck's house, on the doorstep of which he happened to be sitting.

Black Pussy looked up at Sammy Jay and snarled at him in a terrible rage. Sammy shrieked at her just as angrily. Then, when her head was turned for just an instant, he darted down and actually pulled a tuft of hair from her coat, and was safely out of the way before she could turn and spring. Then Black Pussy thrust a paw down between the stones where Chatterer had disappeared. She pulled it out again with a yowl of pain, for sharp little teeth had bitten it. Slowly and sullenly Black Pussy turned and limped back toward Farmer Brown's house. She suddenly remembered that saucer of milk, and that that was really all the breakfast she wanted.

VII
Chatterer Works Hard

WHEN Chatterer had left the Green Forest because of his terrible fear of Shadow the Weasel, he had been fat. At least, he had been fat for him. All through the pleasant fall, while he had been gathering his supply of nuts and seeds to store away for the winter, he had eaten all he could hold and had filled his red coat out until it actually felt too tight. But now that same red coat hung so loose on Chatterer that it looked too big for him. Yes, Sir, Chatterer had grown so thin that his coat actually looked too big for him. And he was growing thinner every day.

You see, most of the food had been collected and stored away long ago, and Chatterer had to run about a great deal and hunt very hard to find enough to eat day by day, while as for filling a new storehouse—that seemed impossible! Still Chatterer kept trying, and day by day he managed to add a little to the supply of seeds. But it was pretty poor fare at best. There were no plump nuts or tasty pine seeds, such as filled his storehouses in the Green Forest, because no nut or pine trees grew near the Old Orchard, and Chatterer didn't dare go back to the Green Forest for fear that

Shadow the Weasel would find him and track him to his new home. So he patiently did his best to find food close at hand. But it was discouraging, terribly discouraging, to work from sunup to sundown, running here, running there, running everywhere, until he was so tired he was ready to drop, and knowing all the time that the snow might come any day and bury what little food there was. Oh, those were hard days for Chatterer the Red Squirrel, very hard days indeed.

One morning he started very early and made a long journey by way of the old stone wall and the rail fences down to Farmer Brown's cornfield. Of course, Farmer Brown had long ago taken away the corn, but in doing it, a great many grains had been scattered about on the ground, half buried where they had been trodden on, hidden under leaves and among weeds and under the piles of stalks from which the ears had been stripped. For the first time for days Chatterer felt something like cheer in his heart, as he scurried about hunting for and finding the plump, yellow grains. First he ate all he could hold, for he saw that then there would be plenty to take home. Then he stuffed his cheeks full, scrambled up on the rail fence, and started for his new home in the Old Orchard.

"It is a terrible long way to have to carry all my supplies," thought he, as he sat up on the top of a post to rest. "I don't see how I ever can do it. Well, I certainly can't, if I sit here all day!" With that, he jumped down to the rail below him. He was halfway across when he noticed a crack in it. It looked to him as if that rail were hollow part way. A great idea came to him. His eyes grew bright with excitement. He ran the length of the rail and back again, looking for an opening. There was none. Then, very slowly and carefully, he worked his way back, stretching his head over so that he could look underneath. Almost over to the next post he found what he had so hoped to find. What was it? Why, a knothole. Yes, Sir, a knothole that opened right into the hollow in the rail. It wasn't quite big enough for Chatterer to squeeze through, but that didn't trouble him. He emptied the corn from his cheeks and then he went to work with those sharp teeth of his and in a little while, a very little while, that knothole was plenty big enough for Chatterer to slip through.

His eyes snapped with pleasure as he explored the hollow rail. "I'll make this my storehouse!" he cried. "I'll fill it full of corn, and then when I am hungry in the winter, I can run down here and fill up. It will be a lot better than trying to carry the corn up to the Old Orchard." And with that, Chatterer began the work of filling the hollow rail with corn.

VIII
Sammy Jay Drops a Hint

WHATEVER faults Chatterer the Red Squirrel may have, and they are many, laziness is not one of them. No, Sir, there is no laziness about Chatterer. When he has work to do, he does it, and he keeps at it until it is finished. Every morning he got up with the sun and raced along the old stone wall and the rail fences down to Farmer Brown's cornfield, where he first ate his breakfast, and then worked to fill the hollow rail of the fence which he had made into a storehouse. It was hard work, because he had to do a great deal of hunting for the corn; and it was exciting work, because he had to keep his eyes and ears open every minute to keep from furnishing a dinner for someone else.

Redtail the Hawk, who had not yet gone South, discovered him one morning, and Chatterer dodged behind a fence post just in time. After that, Redtail was on hand every morning, watching from the top of a tree for Chatterer to grow careless and get too far from shelter.

Then one morning Reddy Fox surprised him at the edge of a heap of cornstalks. Chatterer had just time to wriggle his way to the middle of the heap. Reddy had seen him, and he could smell him. Very

28

softly Reddy tiptoed around the pile of cornstalks to see if Chatterer had come out on the other side. Then he came back to where Chatterer had gone in, and excitedly began to dig, making the dry stalks fly right and left. He made so much noise that Chatterer felt sure that he wouldn't hear him move, and he didn't. By the time Reddy had worked his way to the middle of the pile, Chatterer was safe in his storehouse in the hollow rail. He had slipped from under the cornstalks, run across to another pile, worked his way through this, and so reached the fence.

After that, Reddy Fox came every morning, hoping to surprise Chatterer. But Chatterer felt quite equal to fooling Reddy and Redtail. Of course, they interfered with his work and were very bothersome, but he wasn't afraid of them. The one thing he did fear was that Shadow the Weasel would hear where he was. That thought bothered him a great deal.

One morning Sammy Jay just happened along. He saw Reddy Fox creeping up behind some bushes at the edge of the cornfield, and at once Sammy began to scream as he always does when he thinks he can spoil Reddy's hunting. Reddy looked up at him and showed all his long teeth, but Sammy only grinned and screamed the louder. Then Reddy walked away with a great deal of dignity, for he knew that it wasn't the least use to try to hunt while Sammy Jay was about. When he had dis-

HARRISON CADY

Then he came back to where Chatterer had gone in,
and excitedly began to dig. *See page 29.*

appeared in the Green Forest, Sammy returned to the cornfield, and there he found Chatterer hard at work.

"I'm much obliged, Sammy, for driving that nuisance away; he bothers me a great deal, and I've got to do a lot of work yet to fill my storehouse before it is too late," said Chatterer, as he hurried to the hollow rail with his mouth full of corn.

"Have you moved down here?" demanded Sammy Jay. "I thought you were living up in the Old Orchard."

"I am. At least, my house is up there, but there is no food there, and so I have made a storehouse down here and am trying to get it full of corn before snow comes," replied Chatterer.

"It will be a long way to come for your food every day," said Sammy.

"I know it," replied Chatterer, "but I guess I'm lucky to have any food to come for."

"Pooh!" said Sammy, "I wouldn't work as you do. I'd use my wits a little. If corn is what you want to eat, why don't you go up to Farmer Brown's? It's nearer to the Old Orchard than this, and the corn is all stored ready for you to help yourself. I get all I want there."

IX
Chatterer Screws Up His Courage

EVER since Sammy Jay had dropped a hint about the plentiful supply of corn over at Farmer Brown's and how easy it was to get all that one wanted, Chatterer had been trying to screw up his courage to go see for himself if Sammy had told the truth. Chatterer had spent most of his life in or close to the Green Forest. He had a very wholesome fear of Farmer Brown's boy and his dreadful gun, and he always had been content to keep away from Farmer Brown's dooryard. The truth is, he was afraid to go up there. You see, there were Black Pussy the Cat and Bowser the Hound and Farmer Brown's boy—why, it was a terribly dangerous place!

And yet Sammy Jay went up there every day and didn't seem to be in the least afraid. He even scolded and said impudent things to Farmer Brown's boy. If Sammy dared go up there, why shouldn't he? He certainly was as brave as Sammy Jay! Right down in his heart Chatterer had always thought Sammy Jay very much of a coward. Yet here was Sammy going up there and helping himself to corn, just as if it belonged to him. Chatterer thought how hard he worked every day to fill that storehouse in the hollow fence rail, and how every minute of the time he had to watch out for Redtail the Hawk and Reddy Fox. It seemed as if he never, never could get enough corn to keep him all winter. And then it was a long way to go every day from the Old Orchard down to the cornfield. Chatterer sighed at the thought.

"If Sammy Jay told me the truth, and it is so easy to get all the corn one wants over there at Farmer Brown's, it will be ever so much easier in bad weather," thought Chatterer. "Anyway, it won't do any harm to have a look and see for myself how things are."

So Chatterer started running briskly along the old stone wall which led right up to Farmer Brown's yard. As he drew near, he would stop every few steps to make sure that the way was clear. At last he reached the very end of the wall, and hiding between two stones, he peeked out. Right across a wide road was Farmer Brown's house, and in the sun on the back doorstep sat Black Pussy, dozing. Chatterer had hard work to hold his tongue. The very sight of her made him so angry that he almost forgot that he didn't want to be seen. He just longed to tell her what he thought of her. But he kept still and set his sharp little eyes to discover where Farmer Brown kept his corn. He could see Bowser the Hound fast asleep in front of his own special little house. He could see the big barn and the henhouse and the shed where the wagons were kept and the long woodshed.

"I wonder," said Chatterer to himself, "I wonder if that corn is kept in any of those places, and how Sammy Jay gets it if it is."

Just then Farmer Brown's boy came out of the barn. Chatterer dodged back at sight of him. He wanted to scold, just as he had wanted to scold at Black Pussy, but he wisely held his tongue. Farmer Brown's boy didn't even look toward him but went straight over to a queer little building standing high on four legs and with wide cracks between the boards of the walls, through which something yellow showed. Farmer Brown's boy went up several steps and opened a door. Chatterer gave a little gasp. There was the corn, more corn than he ever had seen in all his life, more corn than he had supposed the whole world held! Chatterer made up his mind right then and there that he was going to have some of that corn in spite of Black Pussy and Bowser the Hound and Farmer Brown's boy. The very sight of it screwed his courage up till he felt brave enough to dare anything.

HARRISON CADY

Farmer Brown's boy didn't even look toward him.
See page 34.

X
Chatterer Studies a Way To Get
Farmer Brown's Corn

CHATTERER could think of but one thing—
Farmer Brown's house full of corn, and how he
could get some of it. Sammy Jay had said that he
got all he wanted, and Chatterer made up his mind
that he would see how Sammy did it.

So, very early the next morning, Chatterer was in
his hiding place between the stones of the old wall.
Just as Mr. Sun shot his first red rays in at the win-
dows of Farmer Brown's house, Sammy Jay
arrived. For a wonder he made no noise. Chatterer
noticed this right away. Sammy peered this way
and that way, without making the least sound.
When he was quite sure that no one was about, he
flew over to the queer little house on four legs,
where Farmer Brown kept his corn, and thrust his
bill in between the wide cracks of the wall. In this
way he helped himself to all the corn he wanted
without the least bit of trouble. When he had
enough, he flew away as quietly as he had come.

Chatterer grinned. "Sammy has taught me something, although he doesn't know it," said he to himself. "He's stealing that corn, and he doesn't think

it safe to be found out. I must be just as careful as he is."

There were no signs of anyone around Farmer Brown's house. Chatterer scurried across the yard as fast as his little legs would take him straight for the little house. There he found a great disappointment. He couldn't get up to the cracks through which Sammy Jay had helped himself to corn. You see, the little house stood on four stone legs, and before it had been put on those four legs, an old pan had been placed bottom up on each leg. It would be the hardest kind of hard work to climb one of those stone legs, anyway, and even if he did succeed in climbing it, there was no way of getting around that tin pan at the top, and of course he couldn't gnaw through it. Chatterer ground his teeth with anger. It was so terribly provoking to be so near such a feast and still not be able to get to it. He wished he had wings like Sammy Jay.

Chatterer was so intent on studying out some way to get at that corn that he quite forgot everything else. The rustle of a leaf made him turn his head. Goodness gracious! There was Black Pussy within two jumps of him, and her eyes were yellow with fierce desire. Chatterer darted to the nearest tree and scrambled up as fast as he could.

He wasn't the least bit afraid now, because he knew that he could run out on the little branches where Black Pussy would not dare to follow him. So he faced about and he called Black Pussy every-

thing bad he knew of. When she had slunk away,
Chatterer scampered to the very top of the tree to
think matters over, and right then he discovered a
way to get the corn from Farmer Brown's little
house.

XI
Chatterer Grows Reckless

CHATTERER saw that a branch of the very tree he was sitting in stretched right over the roof of the little house and the very tips of some of the twigs actually touched it.

Chatterer's eyes danced. "If I can't get in from the ground, perhaps I can get in from the air," said he and chuckled. Chatterer looked around hastily to see if anyone was watching. No one was in sight but Black Pussy, watching him from the ground. He didn't mind her up there so he ran lightly out along the branch over the roof of the little house and jumped on to it. Swiftly he ran around the edge of it, peeping over. He was looking for an opening big enough to crawl through.

At last, over in one corner, he spied a knothole close up under the edge of the roof. Chatterer dug his sharp claws into the wood to keep from falling and very carefully crept over until he had safely reached the hole. It wasn't quite big enough to push his head wholly through. Gnaw, gnaw, gnaw! The little splinters began to fly. Gnaw, gnaw, gnaw! The hole was big enough, and Chatterer slipped safely inside just as Farmer Brown's boy came out of the house and noticed Black Pussy sitting on the ground, staring up at the roof of the little house.

"Hello, Puss! Did you think you heard a mouse in there?" exclaimed Farmer Brown's boy. "You didn't, because no mice can get in there. Come along over to the barn, and I'll give you some nice, fresh warm milk."

"Phew!" exclaimed Chatterer to himself. "That was a narrow escape! I'm glad that pesky black cat can't tell what she saw!"

When they were out of sight, Chatterer turned to see what kind of a place he was in. His eyes glistened with greed. Corn, corn, corn everywhere! It seemed to him there was corn enough for all the Squirrels in the world.

"And it's all mine!" gasped Chatterer, quite forgetting that he was stealing. Then he began to eat, and he ate and ate until he couldn't swallow another mouthful.

"I believe I'll take a nap right here," said he to himself, and curled up in the darkest corner. In two minutes he was fast asleep, dreaming that all the world seemed to have turned to golden corn and all for him.

"Hello, Puss! Did you think you heard a mouse in there?"
See page 40.

XII
Chatterer Frightens Sammy Jay

CHATTERER the Red Squirrel was mightily tickled with himself because he had found a way of getting into Farmer Brown's corncrib, where was stored so much beautiful yellow corn that it seemed to him that there was enough for all the Squirrels in the world.

The more some people have, the more they want. It is the very worst kind of selfishness and is called greediness. Chatterer had found a way to get all the corn he wanted without working for it, and there was enough to feed him as long as he lived, though he should live to be a hundred years old. To be sure, it wasn't his; it was Farmer Brown's. But Chatterer looked on Farmer Brown and Farmer Brown's boy as his enemies, and he could see nothing wrong in taking things from his enemies. Perhaps he didn't want to see anything wrong. All his life he had stolen from his neighbors. That is one reason they dislike him so. Anyway, if ever a little voice down inside tried to tell him that he was doing wrong, Chatterer didn't listen to it. Perhaps, after a while, the little voice grew tired and didn't try any more.

After Chatterer had made a few successful trips

to the corncrib, he began to look upon it as his own. He would sometimes hide in the old stone wall, where he could watch Farmer Brown's boy open the door of the corncrib and fill a basket with yellow ears to feed to the hens and the pigs and the horses. At such times Chatterer would work himself into a great rage, as if Farmer Brown's boy were stealing from him. But there was nothing he could do about it, so he would go back to the Old Orchard and scold for an hour. But what made him still angrier was to see Sammy Jay help himself to a few grains of corn from between the cracks in the walls of the corncrib. He forgot how Sammy had first told him about the corncrib, and how Sammy had warned him about Shadow the Weasel. That is the trouble with greed: it forgets everything but the desire to have and to keep others from having. Chatterer didn't say anything to Sammy Jay, because he knew it would be of no use. Besides, if he did, Sammy might meet him over in the corncrib someday and make such a fuss that Farmer Brown's boy would find him.

Finally Chatterer thought of a plan and chuckled wickedly. The next morning he was over in the corncrib bright and early. This time he stayed there until it was time for Sammy Jay to arrive. Peeping out of the hole by which he came and went, he saw Sammy come flying from the Old Orchard. Sammy made no noise, for, you see, Sammy meant to steal, too. Presently Sammy found a crack against which an ear of corn lay very close. He began to peck at it and pick out the grains. Chatterer stole over to it, taking the greatest care not to make a sound. Presently Sammy's black bill came poking through the crack. Chatterer seized it and held on.

Poor Sammy Jay! He was terribly frightened. He thought that it was some kind of a trap. He beat his wings and tried to scream but couldn't, because he couldn't open his mouth. Then Chatterer let go so suddenly that Sammy almost fell to the ground before he could catch his balance. He didn't wait to see what had caught him. He started for the Green Forest as fast as his wings could take him, and as he went he screamed with fright and anger. Chatterer chuckled, and his chuckle was a very wicked-sounding chuckle.

"I guess," said Chatterer, "that Sammy Jay will leave my corn alone after this."

XIII
Sammy Jay Tells His Troubles to Reddy Fox

SAMMY JAY could think of nothing but the terrible fright he had had at Farmer Brown's corncrib. He had thrust his bill through a crack for a
few grains of corn when something had seized his
bill and hung on. Sammy didn't have the least bit of
doubt that it was a trap of some kind set by Farmer
Brown's boy. He flew down to the Green Forest to
think it over and plan some way to get even with
Farmer Brown's boy. As he sat there muttering to
himself, along came Reddy Fox. For a wonder,
Reddy saw Sammy before Sammy saw him.

Reddy grinned. "Sammy certainly has got something on his mind," thought Reddy. Then he said
aloud: "Hello, Sammy! What's the matter? You look
as if you had the stomach-ache and the headache
and a few other aches."

"Matter enough, Reddy Fox! Matter enough!"
snapped Sammy. Then, because he felt that he just
had to tell someone, he told Reddy all about his
terrible fright that morning.

"It was a trap," said Sammy. "It was some kind of
a trap set by Farmer Brown's boy. Just as if he
couldn't spare a few grains of corn when he has got

45

"Matter enough, Reddy Fox! Matter enough!"
snapped Sammy Jay. *See page 45.*

so much! I—I—I'd like to—to peck his eyes out!
That's what I'd like to do!"

Sammy said that because it was the most dreadful thing he could think of, but he didn't really
mean it. Reddy knew it and grinned, for he also
knew that Sammy didn't dare go near enough to
Farmer Brown's boy to more than scream at him.
All the time he had been listening, Reddy had sat
with his head cocked on one side, which is a way
he has when he is thinking. Inside he was laughing,
for Reddy knows a lot about traps and about
Farmer Brown's boy, and he didn't believe that
Farmer Brown's boy would ever set a trap in such
a queer place as a crack in the wall of a corncrib.

"He wouldn't bother to try to trap Sammy Jay; he
would just watch with his gun and shoot Sammy if
he really cared about the few grains of corn Sammy
has taken," thought Reddy. "It was someone or
something else that frightened Sammy. But it isn't
the least bit of use to tell him so. I believe I'll have
a look and see what is going on at that corncrib."
Aloud he said:

"That was a terrible experience, Sammy Jay, and
I don't wonder that you were frightened. Are you
going up there tomorrow morning?"

"What?" screamed Sammy. "Going up there
again? What do you take me for? I guess I don't
need but one lesson of that kind. There's plenty to
eat in the Green Forest and on the Green Meadows
without running any such risk as that. No, Sir, you

won't catch me around Farmer Brown's corncrib again very soon. Not if my name is Sammy Jay!"

"You are wise, very wise," replied Reddy gravely. "It is always wise to keep out of danger." And with this, Reddy trotted on up the Lone Little Path, and inside his red head were busy thoughts. Reddy had made up his mind that there was something very queer about Sammy Jay's fright, and he meant to find out about it. He would be on hand at the first peep of day the next morning and see what was going on around Farmer Brown's corncrib.

And all day long Sammy Jay flew about through the Green Forest telling everyone who would listen how Farmer Brown's boy had tried to trap him. Late that afternoon he visited the Old Orchard and told his story all over again to Chatterer the Red Squirrel, and Chatterer didn't so much as smile until after Sammy had left. Then he threw himself on the ground and rolled over and over and laughed until his sides ached.

XIV
Reddy Fox Plays Spy

REDDY FOX didn't have to get up early to be hiding behind the fence back of Farmer Brown's corncrib when jolly, round, red Mr. Sun chased the little stars from the sky. He didn't have to get up early, for the very good reason that he hadn't been to bed. You see, Reddy Fox does a great many things that he wouldn't like to have seen, and so he does them in the night when most of the other little people of the Green Meadows and the Green Forest are asleep. And so it happens that often he does not go to bed at all at night, but sleeps in the day, when most honest people are abroad. He had been roaming about all this night, and now he had come to watch and see what was going on at Farmer Brown's corncrib, and whether or not Farmer Brown's boy had been setting a trap there for Sammy Jay, as Sammy was so sure he had.

Just as the little stars disappeared and the first faint light from Mr. Sun began to chase away the black shadows, Reddy's sharp eyes saw something move over at the corner of the old stone wall at the edge of the Old Orchard. Then a little dark form scampered across the road, and there was the scratch of sharp little claws on the tree growing near the corncrib. Reddy grinned and watched the top of the tree. In a minute the same little form ran out along a limb that overhung the corncrib and nimbly jumped to the roof. It ran along one edge and suddenly disappeared. Reddy guessed right away that there was a hole there. He arose and stretched.

"I thought as much," said Reddy to himself. "I thought as much." Then he lay down to watch again. After a while, out popped the same lively little form. It was quite light now, light enough for Reddy to see the red coat of Chatterer the Red Squirrel.

Chatterer's cheeks were stuffed so full of corn that his head looked twice as large as it really is. He ran along the roof to where the tips of the limb of the tree brushed the roof, climbed into the tree, looked sharply to make sure that no one was about, particularly Black Pussy, and then ran down the tree and scurried across the road to the safety of the old stone wall.

"Ha!" said Reddy Fox, "I thought so! Unless I am much, very, very much, mistaken, Chatterer can tell Sammy Jay what caught him by the bill yesterday morning and frightened him nearly to death. I've wondered why he no longer came to that new storehouse of his that he worked so hard to fill down at the edge of the cornfield, and now I know. My, but Chatterer is getting fat! I think he will make me a very good breakfast. I do, indeed!"

Reddy licked his lips as if he could already taste fat Red Squirrel, and then slipped away in the other direction, for it was getting so light that he dared stay no longer so near to Farmer Brown's house and Bowser the Hound.

All the way to the Green Forest Reddy grinned, partly at thought of the sharp trick he was sure Chatterer had played on Sammy Jay, and partly at thought of the good breakfast he was sure he would have one of these fine mornings, for already he had thought of a plan to catch Chatterer. But first he would find Sammy Jay. He wanted to see how foolish Sammy would look when he found out that it wasn't a trap of Farmer Brown's boy at all that had frightened him so.

XV

Sammy Jay Spoils the Plan of Reddy Fox

REDDY FOX found Sammy Jay in a bad temper. Sammy had missed his usual breakfast of corn stolen from Farmer Brown's corncrib, and it had made him cross.

"Good morning," said Reddy in his politest manner, and no one can be more polite than Reddy Fox when he sets out to be.

"Morning," mumbled Sammy Jay.

"I found out something this morning which may interest you," said Reddy, taking no notice of Sammy's cross looks.

"It won't," replied Sammy positively. "It won't. Nothing interests me."

"Not even traps?" asked Reddy slyly.

"What's that?" demanded Sammy, looking at Reddy sharply.

"Oh, nothing much," replied Reddy, quite as if the matter didn't interest him especially, "only I found out something this morning that I thought you might like to see, if you weren't such a coward."

"Who says I'm a coward?" shrieked Sammy Jay, dancing about with anger.

"I do," replied Reddy. "You don't dare go with me tomorrow morning and see what is going on at Farmer Brown's corncrib."

"It isn't true!" Sammy shrieked. "I dare go wherever you dare go, so there, Reddy Fox!"

"Then I dare you to meet me tomorrow morning at the edge of the Green Forest at sunup and go with me to watch Farmer Brown's corncrib," Reddy replied.

"I'll be there!" snapped Sammy. "I'll have you to understand that you don't dare do anything that I don't dare do!" snapped Sammy, though to tell the truth he had felt his heart sink at the mere mention of Farmer Brown's corncrib, for you remember it was there that he had had a terrible fright only the morning before.

"All right, see that you are on hand at sunup sharp," replied Reddy and trotted away grinning, for he was smart enough to know that Sammy would risk a great deal rather than be called a coward, for no one likes to be called a coward.

Early the next morning Reddy Fox and Sammy Jay met at the edge of the Green Forest.

"Now," Reddy explained, "we will go over by the fence back of the corncrib. I will hide there, just where I hid yesterday morning, and you will hide in the evergreen tree close by. Watch the roof of the corncrib, and I think you will see something that may explain how you happened to be caught by the bill the other morning. But whatever you see, don't make a sound, not the least bit of a sound."

Sammy promised, and they hurried over to their hiding places. Hardly had Sammy settled himself in the evergreen tree when he saw Chatterer jump to the roof of the corncrib from the limb of the tree which overhung it. Almost in a flash Chatterer had disappeared through a hole just under the edge of the roof. No sooner was he out of sight, than Reddy Fox ran swiftly across to the old stone wall at the edge of the Old Orchard and hid behind it. Right away Sammy Jay guessed that Chatterer had had something to do with the terrible fright he had had at the corncrib when his bill was caught as he pecked at the corn between the cracks in the wall.

"It wasn't a trap at all, but Chatterer!" thought Sammy and right away grew so angry that he could hardly sit still. But he wanted to see what Chatterer would do next, so he bit his tongue to keep it still. Pretty soon out came Chatterer with his cheeks stuffed full of corn. That was too much for Sammy Jay. He forgot all about his promise not to make a sound. He darted out of his hiding place and flew at Chatterer in a terrible rage, screaming at the top of his voice and calling Chatterer every bad thing he could think of. Of course, Chatterer couldn't reply, because his cheeks were so stuffed with corn, but he could run. Like a little red flash he was in the tree that

HARRISON CADY

No sooner was he out of sight, than Reddy ran swiftly
across to the old stone wall. *See page 54.*

overhung the corncrib and dodging around the trunk.

Over behind the stone wall Reddy Fox snarled, for with such a noise he knew it wasn't safe to stay there any longer.

XVI
Chatterer and Sammy Jay Quarrel

When people lose their tempers
   Oh, what a sorry sight!
They call each other dreadful names,
   And sometimes scratch and bite.
The Merry Little Breezes ran
   And hid themselves away
When Chatterer his temper lost,
   And so did Sammy Jay.

IT REALLY was too dreadful! It quite spoiled the day for all the little people who were within sound of their voices. You see, when Sammy Jay discovered that it was Chatterer and not a trap set by Farmer Brown's boy that had given him such a fright at Farmer Brown's corncrib, right away Sammy's temper just boiled right over. Chatterer had his mouth so full of corn that he couldn't say a word, but he could run; and run he did, scampering across Farmer Brown's dooryard to the shelter of the old stone wall at the edge of the Old Orchard with Sammy after him, screaming "Thief! thief! thief!" at the top of his lungs.

"My gracious, what a racket!" exclaimed Farmer Brown's boy, as he opened the door. "That Jay is making such a fuss that I should think there was a fox about." He put his milk pails down and stepped back into the house. In a minute he was out again, with his terrible gun in his hands. He went straight to the old stone wall where only a few minutes before Reddy Fox had been hiding, and it was well for Reddy that he had slipped away the minute Sammy Jay began to scream at Chatterer. Farmer Brown's boy looked disappointed when he saw no signs of Reddy. Then he went over to the little house of Bowser the Hound and unchained Bowser.

Bowser wagged his tail and yelped with delight when he saw the gun, for he dearly loves to hunt. He ran ahead back to the Old Orchard, and almost at once his great, deep voice told all within hearing that his wonderful nose had found the tracks of Reddy Fox.

"I thought so," said Farmer Brown's boy. "I thought there had been a fox here." Then he sighed, for he would have liked nothing better than to go hunt for Reddy. But there were the empty milk pails, and Farmer Brown's boy is not the kind who run away for pleasure when there is work to be done.

Sammy Jay had flown away as soon as he saw Farmer Brown's boy and his terrible gun. Chatterer had hidden in the old stone wall, where he safely stored away the corn with which his cheeks had been stuffed. As soon as Farmer Brown's boy had gone to the barn to milk the cows, Sammy Jay slipped back to the Old Orchard to look for Chatterer, and his temper hadn't improved a bit. He soon saw Chatterer running along the old wall and once more began to scream "Thief! thief!" And now that his mouth was empty, Chatterer could reply, and you know Chatterer has one of the worst tongues of all the little people in the Green Forest.

"Thief yourself!" he screamed back. "Thief yourself! You stole my corn!"

"It isn't your corn any more than it's mine!" screamed Sammy. "I told you about it in the first place. Thief! thief! thief!"

And from that, they fell to calling each other worse things. The Old Orchard never had heard such a quarrel, never. It was dreadful! All day long they kept it up. Twice Farmer Brown's boy came down to see if that fox had come back, and scratched his head, and wondered what all the fuss was about. At last Sammy Jay had a thought.

"I'm going straight over to the Green Forest to tell Shadow the Weasel where you are living!" he cried suddenly. "When he finds you, you won't steal any more corn or be so greedy that you won't let other people have a share."

XVII
Chatterer and Sammy Jay Make Up

WHEN Chatterer heard Sammy Jay say that he was going straight to the Green Forest to tell Shadow the Weasel that Chatterer was living in the Old Orchard, a great fear filled his heart. He forgot his quarrel with Sammy. He forgot his greed for all the corn in Farmer Brown's corncrib. He forgot everything but his terrible fear of Shadow the Weasel. It was because of Shadow that Chatterer had left the Green Forest to live in the Old Orchard. If Shadow should find him here, he didn't know what he could do or where he could go. He knew that Sammy Jay meant just what he said, for though it would be a dreadful thing to do, people do dreadful things when they are angry, and Sammy Jay was very, very angry indeed. He had already spread his wings when Chatterer spoke.

"Please don't do that, Sammy Jay," he begged. "I—I—I didn't mean all the bad things I have said."

Sammy Jay's eyes snapped. He saw right away that Chatterer was very much frightened, and he knew that, hereafter, so long as Shadow the Weasel was anywhere around, Chatterer would be so afraid that he would do anything Sammy might want him to. You see, Sammy Jay is very sharp.

"Am I any more of a thief than you are?" he demanded.

"No-o-o," replied Chatterer slowly, as if it were the hardest work to say it.

"Will you play any more tricks on me?" asked Sammy.

"No," replied Chatterer more promptly this time.

"Well, I'll think it over and make up my mind in the morning," said Sammy. "Perhaps I will and perhaps I won't tell Shadow where you are living. I'll think it over."

Now Sammy knew perfectly well that Chatterer wouldn't sleep a wink that night for worrying. Already he had made up his mind not to tell Shadow, for like all the other little meadow and forest people, he hated Shadow. But, of course, Chatterer couldn't know that he had so made up his mind, and a great fear that Sammy might tell clutched his heart.

"If you'll promise not to tell Shadow where I am, you—you are welcome to all the corn you want at Farmer Brown's corncrib," said Chatterer in a very meek voice.

"Indeed!" replied Sammy. "How very generous of you, seeing that it doesn't belong to you, anyway, and I have just as much right to it as you have."

"And—and—well, I'll help you get it," continued Chatterer, his sharp wits working their hardest to think of some way to get Sammy to make that promise.

Harrison Cady

"No-o-o," replied Chatterer slowly. *See page 61.*

"How?" asked Sammy suspiciously.

"Why, when you can't get it between the cracks, I'll bring some out for you and hide it in the stone wall where you can find it," replied Chatterer. But in his heart he said that he would hide it so that Sammy would have to hunt a long time to find it. It seemed almost as if Sammy read that thought, for, cocking his head on one side, he said:

"I'll promise not to tell Shadow, if you'll promise to get me corn whenever I want it and put it just where I tell you to."

Chatterer didn't like that idea at all, but what could he do? He thought it over so long that Sammy Jay spread his wings as if to start that very instant for the Green Forest.

"I promise!" cried Chatterer hastily.

And so these two scamps of the Green Forest made up and planned how they would live all winter on Farmer Brown's corn.

XVIII
Chatterer Has To Keep His Promise

CHATTERER wished now that he hadn't been quite so greedy. If he had been content to let Sammy Jay get what corn he could from Farmer Brown's corncrib, instead of playing that sharp trick to frighten him away, Chatterer wouldn't have had to make that promise to get the corn for Sammy and put it wherever Sammy wanted it put. It wasn't much to do. Chatterer really didn't mind doing the thing itself; it was the thought that Sammy could make him do it.

Now Chatterer has sharp wits, and Sammy Jay has sharp wits. Chatterer had always thought his the sharpest, and it hurt his pride to feel that Sammy had got the best of him. He couldn't think of anything else as he curled up for the night in his snug bed in the old home of Drummer the Wood-pecker up in the Old Orchard. He thought and thought and thought and thought, trying to find some way to wriggle out of his promise, and just before he fell asleep, an idea came to him. He would go over to the corncrib before Sammy Jay was awake, eat his fill, and then hide from Sammy.

"Why didn't I think of that before?" he mur-

mured sleepily and smiled to think how, after all, his wits were sharper than those of Sammy Jay.

The next morning, very early, Chatterer visited the corncrib, ate a hurried breakfast, and then hid in the old stone wall to watch for Sammy Jay. But Sammy didn't come at the time he used to visit the corncrib before Chatterer had given him that terrible scare. Chatterer waited and waited, but no Sammy Jay. Chatterer began to get impatient, but still he didn't dare leave his hiding place for fear that Sammy might come. At last Chatterer decided that Sammy had gone somewhere else that morning, so he came out of his hiding place and frisked along the stone wall at one edge of the Old Orchard. After a while he forgot all about Sammy Jay. Anyway, he was sure that Sammy wouldn't think of going to the corncrib so late in the morning, for it wouldn't be safe at all. Farmer Brown's boy would be almost sure to see him. So Chatterer forgot his troubles and frisked about and had a splendid time all by himself.

Right in the midst of it, Sammy Jay arrived in the Old Orchard.

"Good morning, Chatterer," said he. "I fear I am a little late for breakfast."

"Breakfast!" sneered Chatterer. "Breakfast! Why, it's nearer dinnertime. I had my breakfast hours ago."

"I thought likely," replied Sammy, and there was a mischievous look in his sharp black eyes, "but I was rather tired this morning, and as long as I hadn't got to go way over to the corncrib myself, I thought I wouldn't hurry. I suppose you have plenty of corn ready for me here."

"Corn ready for you? I should say not!" snapped Chatterer. "You didn't say anything about getting corn for you this morning."

"Didn't I? Well, I guess I must have forgotten to. Never mind—you can run over there and get some for me now," replied Sammy.

"Go yourself!" snapped Chatterer.

"I think I'd rather not," replied Sammy. "Farmer Brown's boy is chopping wood right close by the corncrib, so I prefer to have you go."

"I won't!" Chatterer fairly screamed and danced about in his rage. "I won't!"

"Oh, all right," replied Sammy, yawning. "I saw Shadow the Weasel down in the Green Forest this morning, and he inquired for you. I think I'll go look him up again."

Chatterer turned pale. He feared Shadow the Weasel more than anyone else under the sun. He would rather face Farmer Brown's boy. "I—I'll go," he stammered weakly. There was no way out of it; he just had to keep his promise.

XIX
Chatterer Gets Sammy Jay Some Corn

IN ALL his life Chatterer had never felt so angry and so helpless. He had thought himself so smart that he could outwit Sammy Jay, and instead Sammy had outwitted him. This was bad enough in itself, but to make matters worse he had to do something which he felt was very dangerous. He had to get Sammy some corn from Farmer Brown's corncrib right in broad daylight, and there was Black Pussy sitting on the doorstep of Farmer Brown's house, and Farmer Brown's boy himself was chopping wood close by the corncrib. But if he didn't keep his promise, Sammy would go tell Shadow the Weasel where he was living, and Chatterer was more afraid of Shadow than of Black Pussy and Farmer Brown's boy. Wasn't it a terrible position to be in? Chatterer thought so. And all the time he knew that it was all his own fault. If he hadn't been so greedy and tried to scare Sammy Jay away from the corncrib, he wouldn't be in such a fix now.

He ran along the stone wall to the end at the edge of Farmer Brown's dooryard. Then he peeped out. Black Pussy was dozing on the doorstep. Her eyes were closed. Chatterer started across for the

HARRISON CADY

He ran along the stone wall at the edge
of Farmer Brown's dooryard. *See page 67.*

tree close by the corncrib, and then his courage failed, and he ran back to the stone wall. Three times he did this, and each time he looked up to see Sammy Jay grinning at him from an apple tree in the Old Orchard. It was very plain to see that Sammy was enjoying Chatterer's fright. Chatterer almost cried with fear and anger.

The fourth time he gritted his teeth and kept on running as fast as he knew how. He was almost past Black Pussy when she opened her eyes. In a flash she was after him. Chatterer reached the tree first and was up it like a little red streak. There he felt safe. At least, he felt safe from Black Pussy, for she wouldn't dare follow him out on the small branches. But Farmer Brown's boy had seen her rush across to the foot of the tree, and now he stopped chopping wood to watch Black Pussy glaring up at Chatterer.

"What are you so interested in, Puss?" asked Farmer Brown's boy. He couldn't see Chatterer, because Chatterer was smart enough to keep on the other side of the tree trunk. "Is it something you want me to see?" he continued, and started to walk over to the tree.

Chatterer's heart was beating terribly with fright—thump, thump, thump! At just that minute there was a great racket over in the Old Orchard.

"Thief! thief! thief!" screamed Sammy Jay, making a great fuss. Farmer Brown's boy turned to look in that direction.

"I wonder if that fox is prowling around again," said he. And while he was still looking and wondering, Chatterer dropped to the roof of the corn-crib and slipped inside, through the hole he had found under the edge of the roof. He gave a great sigh of relief.

"I believe Sammy Jay did that purposely to make Farmer Brown's boy look over there instead of up in the tree," he muttered. And he was right. Sammy had no desire to have any real harm come to Chatterer, and so at just the right minute he had fooled Farmer Brown's boy, just as he often had fooled him before by screaming as if he saw Reddy Fox, when Reddy wasn't there at all.

When Farmer Brown's boy was sure that Reddy was not over in the Old Orchard, he once more turned to Black Pussy, who was still glaring up at the place where Chatterer had been. He looked up, too, but, of course, there was no one to be seen.

"I guess you must have dreamed you saw something, Puss," said he, stooping to stroke her gently. Then he went back to his wood-chopping. Black

Pussy waited a few minutes longer and then went over to the barn to try to console herself with a mouse. Chatterer watched his chance and got back to the old stone wall safely, with his cheeks stuffed full of corn for Sammy Jay.

XX
Chatterer Remembers Something

CHATTERER was disgusted with himself, with all his neighbors, and with the world in general, which is to say that Chatterer was very much put out about something. There was no doubt about it. He couldn't see anything cheerful in the sunshine nor anything pleasant in the blue, blue sky, and when anyone fails to see cheerfulness in the sunshine or to find something pleasant in the blue, blue sky, there is something wrong in his own heart. That was the trouble with Chatterer. There was a great deal wrong in his heart.

In the first place, it was filled with anger, and anger, you know, will take all the joy and pleasantness out of anything. And then Chatterer was mortified. He was both angry and mortified because Sammy Jay had proved to have smarter wits than he had. So, as soon as he could do so without being seen, he slipped into his new home in the old house of Drummer the Woodpecker in an apple tree in the Old Orchard, and there he sulked for the rest of the day. You see, Sammy Jay had made him go over to Farmer Brown's corncrib and get him some corn right in broad daylight, and he had very narrowly escaped being seen by Farmer Brown's boy.

"If only I hadn't promised to get him corn when-ever he asks me to!" he said over and over to him-self, as he sulked in his home in the apple tree. "If only I hadn't! And yet I couldn't help myself—I just had to. Now whenever he feels like it, he'll make me do as he did today and perhaps I won't always be so lucky. Oh dear; oh dear; I've got myself into a dreadful mess, and I've just got to think of some way out of it."

So all the rest of the day he thought and thought, and the more he thought the more unhappy he grew. It wasn't until just as he was going out for a breath of air before going to bed for the night that the great idea came to him.

"Stupid, stupid, stupid!" he muttered, meaning himself. "Why didn't I remember it before? You won't see me going over to that corncrib again, Mr. Jay! I'll get you the corn if I must, but you won't have the fun of laughing at me trying to dodge Black Pussy and Farmer Brown's boy. You're smart, Mr. Jay! You're smart, but you've got to get up early in the morning to play such a trick on Chatterer twice."

Right away he felt so much better in his mind that he had a brisk run along the old stone wall and then turned in for a good night's sleep. The next day Sammy Jay appeared in the middle of the forenoon and demanded more corn. Chatterer pre-tended that he didn't dare go for it, but when Sammy insisted that he must, he suddenly started for—where do you think? Why, for that storehouse of his in the hollow rail at the edge of the cornfield. It was a long way to go, but that was better than running the risk of being seen by Farmer Brown's boy. It took him some time, but at last he was back with his cheeks stuffed with corn. Sammy Jay pretended to be cross because he had been kept waiting so long and grumbled all the time he was eating. He pretended to think that the corn was not as good as that from Farmer Brown's corncrib and mumbled something about telling Shadow the Weasel if Chatterer didn't get him some corn from the crib the next day.

"You can't!" cried Chatterer in triumph. "You promised not to tell Shadow if I kept my promise and got you corn whenever you asked for it; but I didn't say where I would get it," and he chuckled to think that he had been smarter than Sammy Jay.

Sammy ate every grain and then went off, but as he went, Chatterer thought he heard something very like a chuckle. It made him thoughtful and a little uneasy, but he couldn't think of any way Sammy could get the best of him now, so he soon forgot it, and all the rest of the day he thought of how lucky it was that he had remembered that storehouse in the hollow rail.

XXI
Sammy Jay Makes a Call

SAMMY JAY hadn't had so much fun for a long time as he was having at the expense of Chatterer the Red Squirrel. No, Sir, Sammy hadn't had so much fun for as long as he could remember. You see, he and Chatterer never had been very good friends and always had played sharp tricks on each other whenever they had the chance. Sammy had not forgotten how Chatterer had stolen the eggs of Drummer the Woodpecker in the spring and then laid the blame on him, so that all the birds of the Old Orchard had driven him out until they discovered who the real thief was. Sammy had never forgotten or forgiven that sharp, mean trick. And now he was getting even. Right down in his heart he didn't want any real harm to come to Chatterer, but he did love to see him frightened. But his greatest fun was in matching his wits against those of Chatterer, for you know both have very sharp wits, as scamps are very apt to have.

Now all the time he had been mumbling and finding fault with the corn Chatterer had brought from his storehouse in the hollow rail on the edge of the cornfield, Sammy had only been pretending. You see, he had thought of that storehouse before

Chatterer had and had thought Chatterer very stupid not to have remembered it in the first place.
Now that Chatterer had remembered it, Sammy
was glad, although he pretended not to be. Why
was he glad? Well, you see, he knew that Chatterer
was greatly tickled inside because he thought that
he had proved himself smarter than Sammy, and
all the time Sammy saw another chance to prove to
Chatterer that he wasn't so smart as he thought
himself.

When he left Chatterer, he flew straight to the
Green Forest and from there to the edge of
the Green Meadows. His sharp eyes searched the
Green Meadows until they saw his cousin, Blacky
the Crow. Sammy flew straight over to where
Blacky was sitting. For a few minutes they talked
together, and then both looked over to a tall, lone
tree out in the middle of the Green Meadows, in the
top of which sat a black form very straight and
very still. In fact, to eyes less sharp than those of
Sammy Jay and Blacky the Crow, it would have
looked very much like a part of the tree. It was
Roughleg the Hawk watching for Danny Meadow
Mouse.

"Will you do it?" asked Sammy. "I don't dare to
myself because he might have a notion that a fat
Jay like me would make him a good dinner."

"Of course, I'll do it," replied Blacky. "Old Roughleg never bothers me, and it will be a great joke."

"All right," replied Sammy. "Be on hand where

Sammy flew straight to where Blacky was sitting.
See page 75.

you can see what happens tomorrow morning." And with that, Sammy Jay flew back to the Green Forest where he could watch.

In a few minutes Blacky the Crow flew over near the tree in which sat Roughleg the Hawk. Presently Sammy heard Blacky's harsh voice.

"Caw, caw, caw," said Blacky.

Sammy smiled. It was a signal, and he knew that Blacky had done as he had said he would. Then Sammy flew off to look for some new mischief with which to amuse himself for the rest of the day.

XXII
Chatterer Has a Dreadful Day

CHATTERER was feeling quite like himself, his saucy, impudent self, as he peeped out of his doorway at daylight. He felt that he had got the best of Sammy Jay the day before. To be sure, he had to get corn for Sammy, but he did not have to go to Farmer Brown's corncrib for it, and he knew that it was the fun of seeing him take that risk that Sammy wanted more than he did the corn. He felt that he had been smarter than Sammy, and the feeling made him quite like his old self.

> "Chickaro and chickaree,
>   Who is there as smart as me?
> Chickaro and chickaree,
>   Sharper wits you'll never see."

Now that was boasting; and boasting is one of the most foolish habits in the world. But Chatterer always was a boaster and probably always will be. So he whisked in and out of the old stone wall and said this over and over, while he waited for Sammy Jay to appear. He had not gone over to Farmer Brown's corncrib this morning for his breakfast, because he felt sure that Sammy would come and send him for corn, and he knew that he would have to go. But he meant to go down to his own store-house in the hollow rail on the edge of the cornfield and he could eat his fill there. So he scampered about and wished that Sammy would hurry up, for he was hungry.

At last Sammy came, and just as Chatterer expected, he demanded the corn that Chatterer had promised to get for him whenever he should ask for it. Right away Chatterer started for the cornfield, running along the fences. He always did like to run along fences, and though it was a long way down there, he didn't mind, for it was a sharp, cold morning and the run made him feel fine. As he ran, he kept chuckling to himself to think how smart he had been to think of that storehouse and a way to keep his promise to Sammy Jay without running any risk to himself. He was whisking along the fence on the edge of the cornfield and had almost reached the hollow rail where he had stored the corn. He stopped to sit up on a fence post and boast once more:

"Chickaro and chickaree!
Who is there as smart—"

He didn't finish. Instead, his tongue seemed to stick to the roof of his mouth and his little black eyes looked as if they would pop out of his head. Sitting on a post close to the hollow rail was a straight, black form watching him with cruel, hungry-looking eyes. It was Roughleg the Hawk!

Chatterer gave a little gasp of fright. He whirled around and started back along the fence as fast as he could make his legs go. Instantly Roughleg spread his great wings and sailed after him. Chatterer hadn't gone the length of two rails before Roughleg was over him. With his great, cruel claws spread wide, he suddenly swooped down. Chatterer dodged to the underside of the rail just in time, the very nick of time. Roughleg screamed with disappointment, and that scream had such a fierce sound that Chatterer shivered all over.

How he ever got back to the Old Orchard he hardly knew himself. Ever so many times he just managed to dodge those great claws. But he did get there at last, out of breath and tired and frightened. There sat Sammy Jay, waiting for his corn. He pretended to be very angry because Chatterer had none and threatened to go straight to the Green Forest and tell Shadow the Weasel where Chatterer was living. There was nothing for Chatterer to do but to go over to the corncrib as soon as he had rested a little.

"It's been a dreadful day, a perfectly dreadful day," said Chatterer to himself, as he curled up in bed for the night. "I wonder—I wonder how old Roughleg happened to be sitting on that fence post this morning."

But Sammy Jay didn't wonder; he knew.

Chatterer gave a little gasp of fright. *See page 80*.

XXIII
Chatterer Hits on a Plan at Last

EACH time that Chatterer thought himself smarter than Sammy Jay, he found that he wasn't as smart as he thought he was, and this always made him feel mortified. He just couldn't admit even to himself that Sammy was the smartest, and yet here he was every day bringing corn for Sammy from Farmer Brown's corncrib whenever Sammy told him to, and running the risk of being seen by Farmer Brown's boy, all because he hadn't been able to think of some way to outwit Sammy. Once more after he had such a narrow escape from old Roughleg the Hawk, he had tried going down to his storehouse at the edge of the cornfield, but he had found Roughleg on watch and had turned back. From the way Sammy Jay had grinned when he saw Chatterer coming back, Chatterer had made up his mind that Sammy knew something about how old Roughleg happened to have found out about that storehouse and so been on the watch.

Now all this time, Sammy Jay was having a great deal of fun out of Chatterer's trouble. Each time that Chatterer thought of a plan to outwit Sammy, he would find that Sammy had already thought of it and a way to make the plan quite useless. You see, Sammy used to spend a great deal of his time when he was alone in the Green Forest pretending that he was in the same fix as Chatterer and then trying to think of some way out of it. So it was that Chatterer never could think of a plan that Sammy hadn't already thought of. And yet there was a way to cheat Sammy out of his fun, though not out of his corn, and it really was the fun of seeing Chatterer so worried that Sammy cared most about. Sammy had thought of it almost at once, and it seemed to him that Chatterer was very, very stupid not to think of it, too.

"He will think of it someday, and I don't see any way to upset such a simple plan," said Sammy to himself and then fell to studying some new way to torment Chatterer.

And at last Chatterer did think of it. It was such a simple plan! Probably that was why he hadn't thought of it before. All he had to do was to go over to Farmer Brown's corncrib at break of day, before anyone in Farmer Brown's house was awake, just as he had been doing, only make two or three trips and store a lot of corn in a safe hiding place in the old stone wall. Then, when Sammy Jay demanded corn, he could get it without trouble or danger. He tried it, and it worked splendidly. Sammy Jay got his corn, but he didn't get any fun, and he cared more for the fun of seeing Chatterer in trouble than he did for the corn. So, after two or three mornings, Sammy didn't come up to the Old Orchard, and Chatterer chuckled as he stored up the corn, not in one place, but in several places.

Now while Sammy Jay seemed to have grown tired of corn, he was doing a lot of thinking. He had no idea of leaving Chatterer alone. He had just got to think of some way of upsetting Chatterer's simple plan. It was Reddy Fox who finally gave him the idea. He saw Reddy trotting down the Lone Little Path through the Green Forest, and right away the idea came to him. He would tell Reddy where Chatterer was storing the corn in the old stone wall, and Reddy would hide close by.

"Of course, I don't want Reddy to catch Chatterer, but I can prevent that by warning him just in time. But he will be so frightened that he won't dare go to that place for corn again in a hurry, and so will have to go to the corncrib for it," thought Sammy, and hurried to tell Reddy Fox about the place halfway along the old stone wall where Chatterer had hidden his corn.

XXIV
Chatterer Has His Turn To Laugh

SAMMY JAY had not been up to the Old Orchard for several days, and Chatterer the Red Squirrel was beginning to wonder if Sammy had grown tired of corn. But Chatterer had learned that it is always best to be prepared, and so every morning, when he had visited Farmer Brown's corncrib, he had brought a generous supply back to the Old Orchard and hidden it in several secret places in different parts of the stone wall and some in a certain hollow in an old apple tree. Chatterer couldn't quite believe that Sammy had given up all hope of making him more trouble, so he meant to be prepared.

So when Sammy did appear early one morning, Chatterer was not in the least surprised. He pretended to be glad to see Sammy. In fact, he was almost glad. You see, Sammy had so many times proved his wits to be sharper than Chatterer's, that Chatterer wanted to get even. There was a sparkle of mischief in Sammy's eyes. Chatterer saw it right away, and he guessed that Sammy had some new plan under that pert cap of his.

"Good morning, Sammy Jay," said Chatterer, pretending to be polite. "I had begun to think that you were tired of corn. I have some very nice corn ready for you, the very best I could find in Farmer Brown's corncrib. Will you have some this morning?"

"I believe I will," replied Sammy, also pretending to be very polite. "It is very nice of you to pick out the best corn for me, and the very thought of it makes me hungry. I believe I would like some this very minute."

As he spoke, he turned his head to hide a grin, for, thought he, "Of course, Chatterer will go straight to that hiding place in the stone wall and then we shall see some fun." He glanced hastily in that direction, and he saw a patch of red half hidden behind the wall, and he knew that it was the red coat of Reddy Fox. Reddy was hiding just where Sammy had told him to.

Now Chatterer had been doing some quick thinking. He remembered the sharp tricks Sammy had played on him before, and he didn't have the least doubt that Sammy had planned another. "Of course, he expects me to go straight to that place where he knows I have hidden corn for him, and if he has planned any trouble for me, that is where it will be," thought Chatterer. "I think I'll get the corn from one of the hiding places he doesn't know about."

With that Chatterer ran swiftly out along a branch of a tree he was in, leaped across to another tree and then to a third, the one in which was the hollow in which he had put some of the corn. In a few minutes he was back, with his cheeks stuffed full. Sammy Jay pretended to be very much pleased, but he ate it as if he had lost his appetite, as indeed he had. You see, he was wondering what he should say to Reddy Fox, to whom he had promised a chance to catch Chatterer. He knew that Reddy would think that it was all one of Sammy's tricks. So without waiting to finish all the corn, Sammy politely said good-by and flew to the deepest part of the Green Forest.

"Ha, ha, ha! Ho, ho, ho!" laughed Chatterer, as his sharp eyes spied Reddy Fox trying to creep away without being seen. "Ha, ha, ha! Ho, ho, ho! It's my turn to laugh. Ha, ha, ha! Ho, ho, ho!"

And so for the time being, Chatterer had the last laugh, though Sammy Jay knew well that his turn would come again, if only he were patient. But he had other things to think of. You see, he was very much interested in the adventures of Buster Bear. And if you are interested in them too, you may read all about them in another book devoted wholly to the things that happened when Buster came to live in the Green Forest.

LOVE YOU

Tartan Sau